SAVED

WRITTEN BY SYLVIA MORROW

Cover Designed By Unfortunate Reads

CHAPTER ZERO

CONTENT/TRIGGER WARNINGS

PLEASE READ

This book contains depictions of verbal abuse by a spouse.

I needed to write this. Not everyone is in a space where they can handle it. Please take care of yourself.

The following are the content notes and warnings. If you ever come across anything you feel I have missed, that can cause harm, don't be afraid to contact me.

Verbal abuse by a romantic partner, slipping on the stairs, reference to losing virginity when you were drunk, "sex or die", physical violence between strangers, being self-conscious of one's own physical appearance.

CHAPTER ONE

Kwin

"Maybe this is the time you will find her, short tail," Zef calls out to me, laughing, over the vidscreen. "In the ice mines of Mars."

His ship is traveling alongside mine and, while we will be arriving at our destination in only a few short days, it is nice to have company. Even if the male communicating with me is prodding my insecurities.

"Maybe this is the time you get a haircut and take a shower," I grumble. Zef merely laughs louder.

"Ah, who am I trying to impress? There's no one else on this ship. Only you can see me on that vidscreen."

"And when we arrive at our destination I will be the first one to smell you. If you ever want a *sdaha* you must understand smelling nice and being well groomed are the first steps to–"

Zef cuts me off with a wave of his hand and a scoff.

"I don't care about that *sdaha* nonsense. Love? Only

a weakness," he sits back in his captain's chair with a loud thump.

"I shall never become as jaded as you, Zef," I raise my eyebrow at him.

"A challenge? We shall see."

"Not even if I were on my deathbed would I give up on finding my mate. You will see, Zef. I will find her."

CHAPTER TWO

Meg

It's a normal day.

"Hey honey, I'm making myself a bowl of ice cream. Do you want some?" It's vanilla. His favorite.

"Are you stupid? You know my tooth hurts. I can't have cold on it like that. Why would you offer me ice cream?" he shouts his reply from the living room. My stomach drops when I hear his footsteps approach the kitchen.

"Oh. I'm sorry. I forgot." This happens too often. I just wanted to share something nice with him but I screwed it up somehow.

"You didn't think. You never think about my problems. You only care about yourself. My problems matter too. I pay your bills, remember? Or did you forget that?" He's so close to my face now as he demands his answer that I can see the black crud stuck in his dentures.

"I know you matter. I'm sorry, Fred." I'm shrinking, I can feel it. I'm sure I'll be gone, poof, in no time. Maybe that would be for the better.

"Do you even care about me? No, you don't. You use me for paying bills because you can't do shit." He's right. I'm useless. The incredible shrinking, useless woman.

"I said I'm sorry. I'm really sorry. I just wanted to share with you. I wasn't thinking." *Please stop.*

"You never think, you stupid bitch."

"Please stop yelling. I'm really sorry. I didn't mean it." *Please, please stop.*

"I'm not yelling. Do you want me to yell? I can yell. I can YELL!"

"Please stop."

"Are you crying? Fucking Christ, Margaret. Eat your fucking ice cream. I'm going for a walk. You act like I hit you or something. Fucking crying, I can't believe it."

As soon as the door closes, I wipe my tears away and put the container of ice cream back into the freezer. It's no longer appealing.

The freezer closes and then the house is silent. I let my shoulders fall in relaxation. *Take a breath, Meg. Relax.* Just for a moment. When he's gone is the only time I can really breathe, the only time my body feels loose. Last time I went to the dentist, she said I cracked a few teeth. I told her I must be clenching my jaw in my sleep. It's not just in my sleep.

Okay. Moment's over. I don't want to let my guard down too much when he's only going to be gone a little while. He'll be back and I'll be Margaret, not Meg. When he gets back, he's going to want to apologize, which means he'll want to...

Nausea fills my stomach like lead weights, and the tears threaten to return. The *apology* is worse than the argument. I just can't stand it. How did I get into this life? I used to love being touched, held. This isn't me.

Maybe tonight, when Fred is asleep, I'll read a nice romance novel. Escape into my head for a while. Remember what it was like to feel passion.

The front door creaks open, my eyes close. *Dry the tears, Meg. Just breathe.*

"Hey. I'm sorry for yelling. I should know by now how you are."

My face is ice cold as I force a smile I want to deny with every piece of my soul.

"That's okay, honey. I understand."

"Why don't you come over here and give me a hug? Huh, Margaret? A little kiss?"

Please someone take me away.

Please help me get away.

Please save me.

"Of course, honey."

Save me.

CHAPTER THREE

Meg

Two days alone. I can't believe it. Two entire days all to myself. I haven't had this much time alone in over fifteen years. *Two days.* The one good thing about him, his work ethic, got him a promotion that's taking him on an employee retreat for the weekend.

Gosh, I can get so much reading done in two days. I'm going to take a bubble bath. Heck, I'm going to read in the bubble bath, and no one can stop me.

Maybe I'll call Agnes. I can have her over for coffee. No, I'll go visit *her* for coffee. She only lives down the road and yet I hardly ever get to see her. It'll be nice to get out of the house, do something different for a change.

The phone rings only twice before she picks up.

"Is that Meg? I can't believe it!" She whistles as if it's some miracle and I can't help but to roll my eyes.

"Yeah, yeah. I got two days off from Fred. You wanna have some coffee tomorrow? It's been a while."

"Do I? Of course I want to spend time with my best friend and neighbor! I miss you. You never get away from that piece of-"

"I'll see you at noon tomorrow at your house, Agnes. Bye!"

We end the call with a laugh. I grab a drink of water at the sink and am contemplating what to do next, when–

CRASH!

The plastic cup of water I'm holding falls to the floor with a splash and a *bop* as I shriek in response to the ear-splitting noise in my backyard. It sounds like a terrible car accident, a train wreck even. It couldn't be though, considering I live on a mostly empty plot of land in the middle of nowhere.

The morning sun streams through the glass of the little window on my back door, making everything seem cheerful even as the sounds of *zapping* and *beeping* and all sorts of strange things stream in from outside. *Should I call the police?* I bite my lip as I think about what to do. Fred hates having the police around. He's so paranoid about the government. I don't want him to find out I called them and get mad at me.

My sock gets wet from the spilled water, and I cringe. *Yuck.* I slip it off and as I'm doing so lean closer to the back door. *Screw it.* With one sock on and one sock off, I open the door and take a peek outside.

Holy shit.

There's some kind of strange vehicle crashed in my yard. A weird plane or something.

No. I won't lie to myself and I'm not stupid. I've seen enough movies to know that's not a car or airplane. That's a spaceship. *There's a spaceship crashed in my yard.*

And crawling out of it is a man. An alien, I guess.

The...person...coming out of the ship looks vaguely human. The only differences seem to be furry ears like a cat, and some kind of short, stubby tail, like a bunny. Also, he's about seven feet tall and purple.

And coming straight for me, *oh my lord.*

The alien taps something on the side of his head as he stumbles toward the house. He's holding his side, and I can see a tear in the black clothing he's wearing. Things don't look so good there. I guess we both bleed red.

"Bonjour!" the alien shouts, making a pained face.

Huh? My nose crinkles in confusion.

"I didn't know aliens spoke French," I whisper to myself.

The alien pauses, ear twitching in my direction,

before tapping the side of his head again. His short, dark maroon hair flutters softly with the motion.

"Hello!" he shouts, this time falling to his knees in the long grass with a groan. He looks straight at me, black eyes wide in desperation. "Please, I need help."

I've never been one to let anyone suffer if I could help them, and he really looks to be suffering too. Darn it.

"Okay. I'm coming. Just please don't be one of those people-eating aliens or something."

"I'm glad my translator works so that I may assure you I am not interested in your meat," he forces out through his teeth.

"Well, that certainly sounds reassuring and not terrifying at all."

I tug up the waistband of my blue fleece pajama pants so that the hems don't drag in the dirt and head out the door. He's bent over, panting, clutching his side when I get to him. What I see when I crouch down next to him looks pretty nasty.

"You've got a really bad injury there I'm pretty sure, hon. If your anatomy is anything close to ours, that is. You need a doctor. There's nothing I can do here."

"Please. No doctors. No one else. I'm not supposed to be on this planet. Your governments are hostile to outsiders. You will not tell anyone of my arrival, correct? Please?" He looks up from his wound and into my eyes, pleading.

My heart breaks for him. I don't know what happened but whatever it was he sure didn't mean any harm to me, that's clear. Begging is something I understand and something I take seriously.

"I won't tell anyone, I promise."

When I set my hand on his to console him, he draws in a sharp breath and his eyes open wide. He slaps his hand over mine and stares at me as if I've just done something miraculous. A feeling rushes through my hand, up my arm, through my whole body. A feeling like a warm bath, a soft blanket, a crackling fire in winter. It's wonderful but frightening in its intensity. I try to pull away, but I'd have better luck trying to pull a tractor with my teeth.

"Um, can I get my hand back, please?" I ask.

"You are healing me," he says softly.

"I'm what? How am I healing you? I'm just touching you."

"Yes. Exactly. That is what happens when *sdaha* touch one another." He's still speaking quietly, eyes wide, as if in awe.

"*Sdaha*? What's that mean?" I cock my head to the side in question.

"It means I was destined to land here. To find you. It means we are meant to be together."

CHAPTER FOUR

Kwin

My mate is wearing only one sock. I do not know if this is tradition or fashion, but somehow it fascinates me. Will she want me to wear only one sock? I would not like that, but I would do it for her.

"Did you hit your head? I can get you some ice." My mate looks into my eyes with concern. "I can't really tell if your pupils are messed up, since your whole eye is black. Reminds me of a hamster I used to have kinda."

"I do not know what a hamster is. Is it handsome? Brave?" I ask hopefully as the feeling of her touch warms my insides.

"Oh, it's a pet. A tiny little furry thing that lives in a cage."

My hope is dashed.

"And you think I look like one of these pets?"

Her pale, round cheeks turn pink as she quickly responds, "Oh boy, no, I just meant the hamster had black eyes too, that's all. You don't look like one.

Definitely not."

"Ah, good. I'm glad." A sharp pain shoots through my injured side, causing me to hiss and bend over. She is healing me, I know by the glorious warmth of her touch, but the wound is deep. It will take time.

"Let me see that. How bad is it? I should at least get you some clean towels or something." She bites her lip in worry as she looks at the place I hold my torn shirt together.

"I could make use of some bandages. And towels, yes. Clean water as well. Please." I do my best to stand without falling as she rises.

"Um. I'll go into the house now and get those things," she says, pointing to what must be her home.

"Excellent. Let us go."

"Oh, it'll just take me one second. No need for you to put any stress on yourself. Just stay out here and relax," she says with a laugh that sounds nervous.

"Do not worry about me, I am strong. I will join you." I smile at the woman so that she will believe I'm alright, even though I'm in great pain.

"Oh, well, I suppose. Just please don't make a mess. My husband will kill me if he finds out I let a man into our house."

My blood runs cold. *Husband.* Certainly, this cannot be true. My *sdaha* cannot be mated to another. Fate would not be so cruel.

And then I burn with fury. *He would kill her?* My fangs and claws slide out when I think of anyone doing harm to her soft body. *Never.*

"You coming or what?" she asks from beside the entrance to her home. The morning light turns her brown eyes copper, her dark hair gold. Her scent drifts toward me and nearly brings me to my knees when it hits.

"Yes. My apologies. I will be with you," I reply. *I will be with you, my mate, husband, or no.*

CHAPTER FIVE

Meg

Well, there's an alien in my kitchen, sitting right on my kitchen table. He's sexy too, which I did not expect from aliens. I always thought they'd be like those big-eyed gray things. Instead, a big old supermodel with fuzzy animal bits showed up, telling me I'm meant to be with him. Life sure is strange.

"I think we're gonna have to cut this shirt off to see the wound fully. I'm sorry, hon. I'll find you another." I pat him on the forearm, pausing just slightly to enjoy that warmth, before turning around to grab my kitchen scissors out of the drawer.

"It is no worry. Do what you must."

We're silent for a moment as I snip through the fabric before he speaks again.

"I feel like a fool for not asking sooner, but we have not exchanged names. What may I call you?"

"Oh, my name's Margaret, but I prefer to be called Meg. How about you?" I finish cutting off his shirt and...*lord have mercy. Perfection exists and its color is purple.*

"My name is Kwimchimna. I prefer to be called Kwin. But you may call me anything you like, of course, my *sdaha*." He caresses the back of my hand with his and gives me a smoldering look that turns my face red hot and sends lightning up my–

I clear my throat and look away from his face, back to inspecting his side. Guess I'll just keep trying to ignore that scrumptious feeling I get when he touches me.

"I'll call you Kwin then." I check out the wound on his side. It's pretty bad. I may not know alien anatomy, but I know blood loss and this sucker is bleeding. "Alright. Hold these towels against it while I try to search on the internet what to do. You're not, like, poisonous or something weird, are ya?"

"I know what to do, Meg. I need you to hold me. Touch me as much as you can. It will heal me." His eyes follow mine as they dart around the room, trying to escape his gaze. "Please. It is the best possible way."

"Are you sure it's the best way?" I bite my lip in nervousness again.

"Well, the most ideal way would be to mate. If you would be willing to mate with me that would–"

"Touching is fine. Just touching. Above the waist," I

make sure to add that last part. He may be sexy, but I'm still married.

He smirks, a dimple appearing on one violet cheek. "As you wish. And I'm not poisonous. You may touch me freely."

"Where should I touch you?" I swallow my nervousness and wait for his answer. He takes my right hand and presses it gently over the wound.

"Here," he says with pain in his voice. He adjusts me so that I'm fit between his legs, my whole body closer to him than I've been so far. He takes my left hand and stretches it up to lay flat against his cheek. "And here."

My arms are spread apart, and with the way I'm awkwardly positioned my breasts are a little closer to him than I'd like them to be.

Well, *like* isn't the right word. I'd *like* them to be pressed against his face. But that's not okay for a married woman to think about. So, stay away I must.

"That is good. I can feel it working already. Can you feel it, Meg? Can you feel our bond?" His hands settle on my waist. I don't exactly have the smallest waist, but his hands are so big I feel almost petite. I should push him off, but the feeling is just too good.

"I feel something. Not saying it's a bond. You have to understand I'm a married woman, Kwin. It's not proper to just crash into my yard and tell me you want to mate me or whatever. Fred would be so upset with me if he found out." I think about the wrecked ship in the yard and realize there's no way for me to hide that. "Oh no, he's gonna see the ship and know you were here. Shit."

"Meg, it is alright. Do not worry. I have sent a distress signal and I know there is a friend nearby. Someone will come soon. We will take care of things." One of his hands leaves my waist to stroke my cheek. "We will handle your husband problem. Do not worry about him. I am trained in combat. If he attempts to kill you, he will not succeed."

"Oh. Well. That's good to know, I suppose." It seems he took the *he'll kill me* literally. Being honest with myself, maybe I should take it literally too with the way Fred has been acting. I start to feel that familiar nausea creep in, but I shake it off and smile up at Kwin instead.

One of Kwin's ears is cocked downward and the other is up when I look at him. The cocked one turns back around, and I can't help but laugh. He looks at me curiously, ears twitching with emotion, and I laugh even more. *How cute!*

"Are you alright, Meg?" he asks.

"It's just that your ears remind me of a cat. A cat is an animal we have here that people keep as pets. They say 'meow' and they're really cute and sweet," I say. When he frowns, I add, "And they have claws and sharp teeth too!"

"Another pet?" he asks in a low voice. "And what else of me is like a pet? You may as well say now."

I hold my breath for a few seconds to stop my laughter and to think about his question.

"Your tail is like a bunny. Some people keep bunnies as pets," I tell him as I nibble my bottom lip. That lip is getting really beat up today.

"So, I am three times a pet to you. Would you keep me in a cage then?" he grumbles, looking offended.

"No! Of course not." I shake my head.

"Put me on a leash and force me to obey you?"

"No, I would never!" *Though the thought is a little tantalizing.*

"Collar me? Keep me as yours?" he asks much more softly.

"I– No, no, of course not," I say, stumbling over my words.

"Meg–" he starts, but I cut him off. I know he's going to say something seductive, just by the way he says my name and I can't handle it.

"How's your side?" I ask. Back to business.

CHAPTER SIX

Kwin

The device on my belt buzzes. Good. It seems Zef got my call. We were traveling together when I went down so I knew he would still be nearby, I only needed to let him know where I would be.

While I wait, I must convince Meg to leave with me. I will have to move quickly. It's almost certain we'll be caught if we're here too long. One ship entering the planet disguised can be written off as a fluke but two, so close together, will certainly sound alarms.

"It is improving already. Perhaps if you were to remove your top and press your chest against mine, it would–"

"Don't push your luck," she replies, flicking my nipple as she does.

"Ouch! You flicked my nipple!" I gasp incredulously. "Perhaps your kind are different, but for us *Isxiens* it is a very sensitive spot."

"You deserved it. Focus more on healing and less on trying to get into my pants, alright?" she raises an eyebrow at me, and I squint in return.

A raised eyebrow means a challenge where I come from. *Is this her way of slyly challenging me to get into her pants?* I shake my head. No, that is wishful thinking. *Is it?* I will change the topic for now while I come up with a clever way to win her over.

First, I will compliment her. A good male should compliment a female on their attire or talent when first meeting, not their physical body, no matter how distractingly plump and pleasing her body is. I haven't had time to learn much about her talents yet, therefore the decision is made for me.

"I like your sock," I say with a smile as I nod to her only covered foot. Certainly, complimenting her sense of fashion could only help to make her want me.

Meg makes a soft huffing sound while tugging the remaining sock off with her bare foot. When both feet are bare, she looks at me as if I've done something wrong.

"That better? It's not like I lost the other sock in a hurry to come save you or anything. Good to know sarcasm is alive and well throughout the universe." She's visibly upset now, brow wrinkled and face red.

"I do not understand why you are upset with me." My mind races, trying to understand what happened, but I cannot find the answer.

"I'm tired of men being mean to me when I'm

trying to do something nice. I'm standing here helping you, when I could be taking the first time for myself that I've had in years, and you thank me by making fun of me for losing my sock. That's not very nice of you, Kwin. Not very nice at all." She pushes on my wound a bit harder than necessary as she speaks. It takes a lot of strength to keep from wincing when her little fingernails dig into my sliced flesh.

"Meg, I was not insulting you. It was intended to be a compliment. Now, if you would please stop digging your fingers into my wound I would be very grateful." I release a long breath when she loosens her hold on me. "Thank you."

"Oh goodness. I'm so sorry. I didn't mean to do that. It's just that I'm so used to...never mind. Are you getting any better at all? Let me take a look." She looks at the place where I am the most injured and makes a humming sound before covering it again. "I think we can put some bandages on you now and you'll live. That whole speed healing thing is pretty neat."

"I can only do it because of you. Because of our connection."

"Well, you better do all the healing now while you can I suppose. My husband will be back in two days. He left just a little before you crashed so you've got some time, but you can't be here when he gets back. And I can't have anyone seeing that shipwreck.

Alright?" She wipes her hands on a towel as she speaks, then finds some sort of antiseptic to wipe my side. It hurts quite a lot, but I remain still and silent.

While she bandages my side, I take time to think about what she said. Her mouth-watering scent distracts my thoughts; even in my current state it's difficult not to want to caress her every chance I get, even in small ways, but I must focus.

I have two days to win her over. That is plenty of time. There have been many challenges in my life, but I have overcome all of them to get here. Two full days makes this easy. She will be in my arms in no time at all. I will–

A lock turns at the front of the house, breaking the silence.

"Oh no," Meg says, the blood quickly draining from her face. "He's back."

CHAPTER SEVEN

Meg

"Oh shit. I'll try to get him upstairs. You be silent, and then clean up and leave while we're up there. Damn it." I hustle to the front room, hiding my blood-flecked hands in the pockets of my pajama pants. A quick inspection of my clothes shows the blood managed to stay off my pants and that luckily my black shirts seems to be hiding what's there.

The door is opening as I get there, my husband walking through. His sparse blonde hair is wind-blown, and his tie is loosened. It took me forever to figure out how to tie that thing, darn it. Now I'm gonna have to do it for him all over. Well, maybe not; the look on his face tells me the tie is the least of my worries.

"Margaret," he snaps as soon as the door is slammed shut. "Where was my fucking plane ticket?"

Oh no.

"I put it in your coat. I told you." I know I told him. I told him so many times that he snapped at me for repeating it too much.

"Then why wasn't it there? Why did I drive halfway across the fucking state to get to the airport only to not find a ticket in my coat? Hmm?" His face is turning so red it's almost purple. I shrink back and toward the stairs.

"Well, where's your coat?" I ask.

"Are you blind? I'm wearing it. And there's no ticket in it!" He tears off his suit jacket and throws it on the floor of the living room.

Oh no.

"Honey, I showed you. It was in your overcoat, not your suit jacket. You told me to put it there. The nice wool one." I know I did what he told me, but I also know he's not gonna give a shit. I take a backwards step up the stairs.

"Why would I want to wear that on the plane? I packed it away!" He's screaming now. This is bad.

"You were wearing it when you left." Tears fill my eyes. I take another step backward up the stairs. I need that alien to get cleaned up and out of here because I don't think I can deal with any other problems today. Not even sure I'll be able to deal with this one.

"People make changes to plans. That's why you don't put tickets in places like fucking coats. I should know better than to rely on you. I missed my plane,

Margaret. Do you have any idea what this is going to do to my position at the company? Do you even care? I don't think you care about anything." He starts to follow me up the stairs as I back up, one step at a time. "Why are you running away? Huh? What the fuck is wrong with you?"

My heel slips on the edge of a stair. I yelp as I slide down several stairs. Fred looms above me, practiced punishment waiting in his hands. I'm just about to apologize, to beg for forgiveness for something that isn't my fault. The same thing I've done a hundred times before.

But then Fred disappears.

With a loud zap, Fred flies over the railing of the stairs and lands on the living room floor. He lays there, still as a statue. In front of me stands Kwin, a smooth, black device in his hand and a stern look on his handsome face.

Kwin returns the device to his belt and walks down to where my husband is lying. He kicks him with the toe of his boot and when there is no response, gives a satisfied grunt and returns to his position on the stair below me.

"Is he dead?" I ask shakily.

"Unfortunately, no," Kwin spits out in the direction of my still spouse. "He will wake and be as he was in approximately two hours. Fortunately, Zef, my friend, will arrive to take us away in one hour. We will have the area clean and be gone before he wakes. Do not worry. We are–"

Kwin topples over, grunting in pain, hands on his side. Panic races through me as I rush over to him, only to see that he's begun bleeding through his bandages.

"Damn. I hope I have time." He laughs, a cough following shortly after. "Maybe worry a little after all."

I smooth back his maroon hair, pet his soft ears, as I think of what I can do to help. The heat building between us feels even stronger yet, but I try to focus on his injury, not my feelings. One problem at a time. The only solution is something I never thought I'd do but is really the best option. I've always been one to help those in need, and I'm not gonna stop now.

"Kwin," I start, my heart racing about a million miles an hour, "Go upstairs, straight ahead, and lay on the bed. Take off your pants. We're gonna mate."

CHAPTER EIGHT

Kwin

"I may have misheard you in the delirium of my pain. Did you say you would like to mate?" My foggy thoughts have suddenly focused sharply.

"Just go before I change my mind. You said this would heal you fast, right? So, let's heal you. Go on, go." She points upstairs and stands to the side.

I stare at her in shock for a moment before following her instructions. What must be the bedroom is directly ahead of the landing. I feel like a youngling as I kick off my boots and lay on the soft bed. Most males my age have mated many times but not me. I am not a virgin, not really, as I had one drunken encounter with a *Rytujnoq* female when I was a lad. I hardly recall it due to time and intoxication. Other than that, I have waited for my *sdaha*. I must admit I am nearly as nervous as I am excited.

"Here we go then," she says with a soft laugh as she steps through the doorway.

She says she is doing this as an act of kindness,

but when she stroked my ears, I could feel her desire through our bond, the intense heat that has begun to burn inside her. What was at first a gentle warmth has become a bonfire already. I cannot wait to see what more it becomes.

However, I am a good male. I would not take a mate without giving her all the proper, important knowledge.

"If you do not desire this, please say so. You may say you do this out of beneficence, but it will be taken as more. It will be a connection of *sdahae*. You must understand that. We will be forever linked." I sigh, laying my hands on my stomach as I wait for her reply.

"What do you mean linked?" she asks with a frown.

"I will feel your emotions. You will feel mine. We will be able to track one another anywhere. Linked." I brush a stray brown hair away from her round cheek.

"And what will happen if you take too long to heal, don't get out of here in time and get caught by the authorities, do you think?" she asks quietly.

"They'll kill me or torture me. Experiment on me. I don't really know. No one they've ever taken has come back to report."

She lays her head on my chest and lets out a long

sigh.

"I said take off your pants," she says.

I laugh softly as she stands at the foot of the bed, tugging her furry blue pants down. Her scent, already strong, now makes my head spin. Sadly, her shirt reaches down so far I cannot see what she has revealed. Damn. I unbutton my pants and tug them down carefully, using my feet to help drag them off, as too much bending is difficult on my side. When I look again at Meg she is still standing at the end of the bed, this time with her eyes locked between my legs, and a confused expression on her face.

"What's wrong?" I ask self-consciously.

"Well. I don't want to be rude, but you don't have a dick. Or anything. So, I don't know what I'm supposed to do here."

"I do, actually. Have a," I clear my throat and run my fingers nervously through my hair, "a *dick*. It's just considered rude to extrude before our partner is ready unless we have built up that sort of relationship already. I'm sorry, this is awkward. Interspecies relationships and such."

"Oh, that's alright. Well, it's okay, you can, um, extrude now. If that means what I think it means. And if this *really* will help, of course." She crawls onto the bed, kneels next to my hip.

Her large, creamy thighs, dimpled and full, make

it very easy for me to extrude indeed. The hidden slit between my legs opens and my cock snakes out, hard and ready. Meg takes a sharp breath at the sight of the large, blue phallus I now stroke beside her.

"Is this alright, Meg?" I ask. I know that by my people's standards I would be considered impressive, but I do not know how I will be received by her.

"It works like here, right? I mean I just get on top and..." She makes a gesture that shows me we indeed do things the same way.

"We could do things in many positions normally, but of course, I am injured now, so yes."

Meg rises higher on her knees and shuffles forward, showing more delicious flesh. But not enough.

"Will you remove your top garment?" I ask, desire racing through me at the thought.

"No. I don't want you to see me. I'm gross. Just pay attention to the feeling, okay,? It'll feel good even if you don't see it." Her face turns sad and my heart crumbles. Whoever has made her feel less than beautiful will be destroyed, I vow it.

"I will change your mind someday," I swear.

"Oh, shush. Now, let's have some weird alien sex."

CHAPTER NINE

Meg

"Meg, it is obvious when I am ready but how do I know when you are? I do not know your anatomy." His eyes lock between my legs as if he could see through the hem of my shirt.

"Well, we get, um, wet down there," I say with my eyes anywhere but his.

"Are you wet now, Meg?"

"Why is that so sexy?" I ask myself, eyes squeezed shut. "Yes, Kwin, I am. I'm ready."

When I take his big, blue cock into my hand, liquid squirts out from pores all along the sides.

"Oh!" I exclaim, releasing him. It slaps his muscular purple stomach with a wet plop before bouncing back up.

"What's wrong?" Kwin asks, concern etched on his brow.

"When I squeezed it, something came out of it. Like a real dense sponge or something. Is it supposed to do that?" I nervously poke it with my finger, and it wobbles back and forth like any human one would.

"Yes, of course. Lubrication. Is this unusual here?" His cheeks have taken on a decidedly pinker tone, and I realized he must be embarrassed. Well now I feel bad.

"It's not the norm here, no, but if it's normal for you, then it's fine for me. I'll just, uh, get back to it then."

I'm better prepared for the feeling when I hold it again. It's not dripping wet or anything, just a little slick. I can see the benefit to it, considering how large he is compared to me. I suppose it's a good thing after all.

With a deep breath, I line us up, slowly rubbing the head of his cock along my center. The wonderful feeling we get when we touch is magnified here and I admit I'm relieved to finally be able to just enjoy it. When I begin to press him against my entrance, the feeling ramps up further. My brow sweats from the heat building inside me. It takes a lot of effort to get him inside me with our size difference, but the lubrication helps immensely. He encourages me in my efforts and that helps quite a bit as well.

"You can do it, Meg. Just a little more and I will be inside you. You've got this, my sweet *sdaha*. Open that lovely cunt for me."

When he finally begins to slip in, we both moan loudly. He fills me beyond full, stretched farther than I've ever been. The heat has turned to an inferno, and we're the flames. I don't even stop to think before I begin to ride him with a passion like I've never felt before. I didn't even know I was capable of moving my body this way. I move like the dancing flames of a fire and I don't pause until I look into his eyes and see the complete awe and adoration in them.

I break apart, slowing as I find my orgasm. Kwin attempts to lift me, to help me along, but I slap his hands away; he can't risk injuring himself. I let my orgasm finish washing through me, then work fast to finish Kwin. It doesn't take long. He hisses loudly and grabs the sheets tightly as his hips raise. When warm, thick, violet liquid starts pouring out of me, I giggle in surprise.

"Wow, that's a lot of cum," I whisper under my breath.

"Uh-huh," Kwin mumbles. I look over to him to see his eyes rolled back and the goofiest smile on his face.

"Well, don't you look happy," I giggle.

"I am in an incredible amount of pain, actually. My side is healing quickly now, and it feels terrible. But I have never felt better. You are wonderful. I did not know sex was going to be that good. I do not really remember the other time I had it."

"What?" I slip off of him and onto the bed. We both

frown at the loss of the connection. "What do you mean 'the other time?' As in, this is the *only* other time?"

"Yes. I cannot wait until we do it again when I am healed. Will that not be fun?" The goofy look is back on his face again.

"I said I would do it to heal you, I didn't say I would do it again, you know." I cross my arms under my chest. Despite how much I may have enjoyed the act, it was not done for pleasure. It was only done to heal. At least that's what I'm trying to convince myself. I don't know how well it's working.

"But you want to. I can feel it. Our connection is forming already. It is slow because my body is focusing on healing but it is there. Can you feel it?"

"No," I lie. The ache in my side and the incredible fullness in my heart tell me that yes, I do feel it. But I'm not ready to talk about that yet. "Hurry up and heal, your friend should be here soon, right?"

"I'm healing rapidly. And yes, soon. We should prepare for his arrival."

The ache in my side is joined by an ache in my chest at the thought of Kwin leaving. Wait, no, it must just be me feeling his feelings for me. I couldn't be feeling anything for him. Could I?

CHAPTER TEN

Kwin

It doesn't take long for my side to heal enough for me to move around safely. Our connection only continues to grow stronger.

"Here, you can wear this. Sorry that I don't have a lot of stuff to fit you. You're so big and tall and my husband isn't so you can't wear his clothes. I'm big but short, as you can see. I did find one oversized sleep shirt that will work." She hands me a soft, black shirt with short sleeves.

"Thank you. Anything is fine. I will enjoy wearing your scent."

Meg blushes at my words as I pull the shirt over my head. When I'm covered, I look down and notice a picture on the front of the shirt. Some sort of adorable, furry creature.

"What is this?" I ask, pointing to the shirt.

"That's a kitten. It's a baby cat," she says as she puts her fingers to the sides of her head in a mockery of my ears. "Claws, fangs, all of that, remember?" I frown.

"One day you will have me in a collar, I'm certain of it." I say it as if it were a negative but honestly...I wouldn't mind.

"Well, I doubt that, seeing as you'll be gone shortly and I won't ever see you again," she says. A burst of pain hits my chest as both of us feel that loss at once.

"It does not have to be that way, Meg. Come with me. Other places are more accepting of interspecies relationships. They are not small-minded like your Earth. You do not have to stay in this life." I gesture out the bedroom door to where her husband is laying at the bottom of the stairs, waiting to awaken in cruelty and rage. "You could be happy."

"I don't know what would make me happy and I'm afraid to leave. I've never been away from Fred in my whole adult life and I don't even know who I am without him. What if I find out I'm just a scared nothing even when he's gone? Just a stupid cow like he says? I couldn't live with myself. At least here I can pretend he's wrong about me." Tears stream from her eyes faster the more she speaks. "You just met me. I've got nothing to offer you. No education, no work history, no money, I can't even drive. I've got nothing."

The despair she feels, the worthlessness, is like it's crushing me from all sides. How has she been able to live this way?

"None of that matters. None of it. What matters

is who you are. And you are wonderful." I embrace her, holding her to my chest even though she refuses to wrap her arms around me in return. "You are the one who chose to help me even when it could have caused you great harm. You have been kind and generous. Offered me your time, your home, even your body, to help me heal. I want to know everything about you forever, but I will not force you to go with me. I will never force anything on you or hurt you in any way. You are my *sdaha* and that is sacred. Please, Meg. I beg you to reconsider."

She wraps her arms around me in return, finally. Inside me, emotions war and rage and gnash their teeth at one another as she fights years of abuse and hatred for a chance to believe she is worthy of a moment of happiness.

"Meg. You have been so strong to put up with him for so long. It is time for you to let someone help. Let me save you."

There is a moment of time where she looks as if some secret has been revealed. A breath shudders out of her as if she had been holding it a long time.

"Save me," she whispers.

She steps back, looks up into my eyes, and sighs. I feel a weight fall away and a lightness like a new day.

"Yeah," she says, "I think I will let you save me."

CHAPTER ELEVEN

Meg

I only pack a small bag. There isn't much from my life I want to keep. I didn't have any family or many friends and there certainly isn't anything sentimental from Fred I want to keep. I even left my wedding ring on the kitchen counter.

We watch as a pickup truck comes roaring down the dirt road to the back of my house, two people inside it. Kwin waves excitedly so I assume one is his friend. My eyebrows raise in surprise when I see that the person driving is one of the few friends of my own, Agnes. Her short black hair flutters in the wind as she sticks her head out of the window and pumps one fist in the air, even as she steers the speeding truck with the other.

"Yeehaw!" she shouts. Yep, that's Agnes.

The truck pulls to a stop next to us, a cloud of dirt making me sneeze. Agnes' door opens and she scurries out and around the front of the pickup, her skinny, denim-clad legs pumping fast.

"Oh my lord, Meg. Aliens. Real aliens. Can ya

believe it?"

"Hardly!" I laugh.

"Are you coming with us? Getting the hell away from Fred?" she asks, a hopeful lift to her brow.

"Wait, you're coming with? How did that happen?" My disbelief in her alien encounter nearly matched by my own.

"It's a long story. I'll tell you in a bit. But I'll say he sure is a grumpy fella," she shuffles in her boots next to me, subtly nodding toward the truck, and whispers into my ear, "and real sexy too."

I can't help the snort of a laugh that escapes me. When the passenger door of the pickup opens and the alien inside walks out, I see what she means though. He's just as tall as Kwin, and has cat ears too, but he's bright yellow and his hair is longer, wild. When he turns to the side to walk to Kwin I also notice he has a long tail, instead of Kwin's bunny tail.

"I bet that tail would be fun," I whisper back to Agnes.

"Meg," she says, hand on her chest in faux shock, "what kind of books have you been reading?"

"Nothing that prepared me for what Kwin's got going on downstairs," I say with a wink. Agnes' eyes fly open wide.

"You did not." She slaps me on the bicep. "Meg Marie Halston, you did not actually do something wild. I can't believe it. Wow. I'm sure jealous."

We both laugh and continue to talk as Kwin and Zef discuss what to do about the crashed ship. Soon they decide and Kwin comes over to tell us the news.

"It must be set to self-destruct. It is beyond repair and, as intergalactic law requires, no part of it can be left for your people to acquire. The self-destruct mode will vaporize it entirely. This means we will all be traveling together."

"Fine with me!" Agnes says with glee as she throws an arm around my shoulder. "Gives me a chance to seduce that big, yellow hunk of a spaceman."

"Did you say something?" Zef says as he walks up to us, wiping the dirt of the crashed ship from his hands.

"Nope. Nothing at all," Agnes says.

"Well, anyway, everyone stand back. This will just take a second, but the ground will shake." Zef holds up one of the sleek, black devices.

We all step back and behind the pickup truck, crouching down low. Kwin does a countdown on his fingers and when he gets to zero, Zef presses the black device. A soft *boom* sound comes from the place where the ship is, but nothing else happens for several seconds. Just when I think nothing *will* happen, the ground begins to shake. And shake *hard.* We hold onto one another for the next ten or so seconds until it ends. When it's done we wait a bit before Zef tells us it's clear to stand. When I look to where the shipwreck was before there's now nothing but a big hole.

"Wow. That was crazy," I mumble.

"And convenient," Agnes says.

"And now we need to leave, as that will have attracted the attention of some type of authorities," Kwin says as he directs us to the doors of the pickup.

Just then, the back door of the house opens and out stumbles *Fred.*

He must have been woken up by the shaking or something. Oh no. Fuck.

"Meg!" he shouts. "What the hell is going on?"

"I'm leaving, Fred," I shout back as I walk to the side of the truck where he can better see me. "And I'm not coming back."

Kwin joins me at my side, wrapping his arm around my waist. Fred stares at him with disgust.

"You're leaving with some...what is this thing? Is this Halloween early or something? This shit isn't funny, Meg. You're going to get yourself killed." Fred says, feigning worry for me. Kwin slides his hand from my waist stepping toward Fred, carefully removing the black device from his waistband. "I knew you were stupid, Meg, but to just leave town with some loony who thinks he's, what, a cat? That's new levels of dumb I didn't think you were capable of."

"Cat?" Kwin says, putting the device back into his waistband with a growl. He lifts his hands, inspects his claws, and raises his head. "Meow."

Next thing I know, Kwin's moved in a flash, Fred has claw marks down the side of his face, and he's on his knees screaming. My mouth drops open in shock as Kwin claws the other side of Fred's face, deep gashes gushing blood.

"Cats have claws, Fred. And sharp teeth." Kwin turns to me. "Should I introduce his throat to my teeth, Meg?"

I do genuinely contemplate it. Fred lying dead for what he's done to me feels like justice but…it's not me.

"No. You got him good enough. He's gonna have to live with those scars forever now." I am not, however, too good not to spit on Fred as he sits there crying and clutching his bleeding face. "Fuck you, Fred. See ya never. Let's go, hon."

"Hell yeah! Eat shit, Fred!" Agnes shouts.

I wrap my arm around Kwin's waist and we head to the truck.

CHAPTER TWELVE

Kwin

Meg was nervous to enter the ship, but she was brave and did so without hesitation. Her face was strong even when I could feel her anxiety pounding inside of me. Her friend, Agnes, jumped into the entryway with a *whoop* of excitement. Zef is going to have his hands full with that one.

Currently, my hands are full with Meg. And I am very, very happy.

There are only two sleeping quarters on this ship and Meg surprised me by choosing to stay with me rather than Agnes. I assumed she would want to take time to get to know me before sharing a bed but I assumed wrong. *Very* wrong.

Meg is lying next to me, talking, in a night dress while I lay in my sleeping pants. She allows me to touch her shoulder and stroke her soft hair as she tells me stories of her childhood. I want to know everything about her, to memorize every detail, so that I may better know how to make her happy. And I will. Make her happy, that is. I swear it.

"What about you? What did you want to be when you were a kid?" she asks me, gently stroking my bicep with the tips of her fingers.

"In love." When she gives me a look that says she thinks I'm joking I continue. "My dad was cruel to my mother. They were not *sdahae*. It made our household a sad place to live. I swore one day I would find my *sdaha* and have a home filled with joy and love. I took jobs traveling the universe to find you, Meg. You were my dream. Now I have you and I'm the happiest male in the universe."

"Well. That certainly gives me a pretty big confidence boost," she laughs. "I'm still nervous though. You could grow to hate me."

"I could not. Not you." I rub my nose against the tip of hers, she giggles.

"I really like you, Kwin," she whispers.

"That just means I will have to work hard until you love me. Then harder still to keep it that way. Tough job."

"Not so tough I don't think," she strokes one of my ears, the back of my neck, runs her fingers down my spine. "Not so tough at all."

When she strokes my tail, my eyes open wide and a growl rips from my throat. *Shit.*

"Oh," she exclaims as she pulls her hand back. "That was…*oh.*"

Her cheeks flame red and I remember that she can feel my strong feelings as well. That will take some getting used to, but in this instance, it's better that I don't have to explain that my tail is an erogenous zone.

Meg presses her body against mine and her breathing increases in pace. Her eyes go half-lidded as I feel her hand snake back down my spine.

"Meg," I warn, "do not start that if you do not want it. Please."

My heart pounds and my cock is so hard it's beginning to extrude on its own. When she closes her hand around the base of my tail and rotates it? I lose control entirely, slapping her hand away and ripping down my pants.

"Oh fuck," Meg shouts as I pin her to the bed, arms over her head, my hips over hers.

"Yes. Fuck," I growl, senses reduced to nothing more than wanting to mate my beautiful *sdaha*. I was tamed by injury before, but now, I'm in my natural state. And I'm *hungry*.

"Um. You're extruded, hon," Meg says and I realize that my cock has fully escaped my slit.

"Yes. Too hungry for you to wait. Impatient." I can barely form sentences. I need her. I'm aching so hard now that I'm leaking lubricant everywhere.

"You're getting my nightgown all wet," she laughs.

"Then take it off. Let me see my *sdaha* as I fuck her into paradise." I release her hands and sit back on my heels, stroking my cock with one hand, waiting for her to undress. She doesn't.

"But I'm...what if you don't like me?"

"Can you not feel how I ache for you? I won't be able to lie to you. Take. It. Off," I snap.

Meg bites her lip, closes her eyes, and pulls her night dress over her head, tossing it onto the floor. She is still wearing her damn undergarments so I frustratedly tear them off as she yelps.

I sit back again and assess the beauty before me. I nearly come from the sight. Soft rolls and a rounded stomach wait for my touch. My cock leaks freely now at the sight of all that flesh waiting. Her soft breasts with their impressive nipples waiting for me to suck. I think of tucking my cock between those tits and rutting away, my cock head aimed to her mouth, watching her drink pints of my release; I drop to my hands and knees in weakness.

"You do like me," she says softly, amazement in her voice.

A quiet laugh leaves me on a wry smile as I look up to face her. "Quite a bit more than like, *sdaha*."

Biting her lip once more, she spreads her legs slightly until I move my arms. She lifts them to her knees and spreads them wide. A feast is laid before me. I crawl between her stretch-marked thighs to closer witness her glory.

"Meg," I rasp, "thank you."

I drag my rough tongue up her center and delight in her soft moan. I plunge it into her depths, first tasting the sweet and salty flavor I know I'll crave the rest of my life. Exploring her further reveals a small bud that proves to be particularly sensitive. Focusing on this area seems to bring her the most pleasure so I continue. I pay attention to her feelings inside of me and it's easy to bring her to her peak.

"Kwin, that was fantastic. That was so good. Please, fuck me. I need you," she whines.

"No need to beg for me. I'm right here. I'll always be here. I love you."

With that, I push inside, stretching her open. I can see her grit her teeth as she takes me all the way. I look down and my cock pulses at the sight of her pussy stretched so wide around me. When she's fully seated, I knead handfuls of her soft breasts, unable to resist the allure.

"I love your breasts. One day will you let me fuck them?" I ask, my breath coming out in short streams now.

"You like them? You don't think they're too– oh fuck, you feel so good," she says, cut off from whatever insult she was going to throw upon herself by the thrust of my hips.

"They're fantastic. Perfect for me. And I'm going to fuck them. And I'm going to fuck your pretty mouth," I thrust hard into her, "and your tight ass," I thrust again as she cries out, "and you'll love every second of it. Now be good for me and take my cock in your glorious cunt and shout the name of the only male who will make you come for the rest of your life."

"Kwin," she says, barely a strangled mewl.

"I said shout it, my holy *sdaha*!"

"Kwin!" she shouts as I ruthlessly pump my hips into her. As she comes around my throbbing cock, "Kwin!"

"Very good," I say with relief as I finally allow myself to come as well. I pour pints into her, lubricant and semen sloshing onto the mattress. There's a reason my kind sleep on waterproof beds.

Meg looks down and laughs uproariously. I lay down next to her, not quite ready to clean up, and watch her with what I'm sure is a goofy grin.

"What's so funny?" I ask.

"I'll just never get used to the river of jizz," she laughs again.

"It makes for fun oral sex," I say, laying my head on her chest and tapping her mouth with a finger.

"Oh. Uh. This ship does have showers, right?" Meg asks.

Now it's my turn to laugh.

CHAPTER THIRTEEN

Zef

The tiny human snores loudly yet again. I cannot sleep. She is louder than a *Xardad* with a head cold. I sleep on the cold floor of my own ship like a stowaway. This room is so small that in the night when her skinny leg falls off the bed, she kicks me in my back.

I love it, nonetheless. One day I will sleep in the bed with her. She does not yet know it, but she is my *sdaha*. The adventures we will have shall be endless.

She does not know the horrors I have lived through or what I would have become without her. She doesn't need to know yet. Right now, I'm content with knowing she's safe. She's near me. And, like Kwin and Meg's love story, she's saved me.

We soon will have our own tale to tell.

THANK YOU

Thank you to all of the beta readers in my Discord server, you were all super helpful! I appreciate all of your help so much! And thank you to Shannon, Cassie, and Latrexa for letting me whine in your inboxes every day. I've discovered that if I can't whine, I can't work, it's just how it is.

Made in the USA
Coppell, TX
23 January 2026